WINFIELD PUBLIC LIBRARY

1/21/21

DISCARD

COW BOY IS NOT A COWBOY

by Gregory Barrington

HARPER
An Imprint of HarperCollinsPublishers

For my Goat Girls,
Haley, Bella, and Leigh

Cow Boy Is NOT a Cowboy

Copyright © 2020 by Gregory Arthur Barrington

All rights reserved. Manufactured in Italy.

No part of this book may be used or reproduced in any manner whatsoever without written permission except in the case of brief quotations embodied in critical articles and reviews. For information address HarperCollins Children's Books, a division of HarperCollins Publishers, 195 Broadway, New York, NY 10007.

www.harpercollinschildrens.com

Library of Congress Control Number: 2019946113

ISBN 978-0-06-289136-5

The artist used pencil sketches scanned and painted in Adobe Photoshop.

On Humdrum Farm, where nothing ever happens, chickens lay extraordinarily average eggs.

Pigs roll in the mud only when necessary, never for fun.

And goats eat very boring food, except for one . . .

Goat Girl.

While a Humdrum goat would be satisfied eating a cardboard box, Goat Girl practiced the art of French cooking.

I present a ratatouille Provençale with a caramelized onion soufflé. **BON APPÉTIT!**

When the Humdrum goats wouldn't play a game of kick the can with Goat Girl . . .

You're NOT supposed to EAT it!

. . . she invented her own game.

Goat Girl's COSTUMES

RAHR!

And when the Humdrum goats closed Lookout Rock over their fear of heights . . .

. . . Goat Girl found
a new solution.

WOO
HOO!

There was nothing humdrum about Goat Girl.

One humdrum day, she saw something new.

Merle actually wasn't new. He was the oldest animal on Humdrum Farm, but he kept to himself.

Every morning.

Every night.

Through every type
of weather.

He was very
humdrum.

Hello, COWBOY!

My name is Merle and
I am **NOT** a cowboy.

Merle was not amused.
He proceeded to explain exactly
why he was NOT a cowboy.

I am not adventurous.
I am not brave.
I might even be allergic to horses.

Things Merle
Will Do:

Sit in a Field

Things Merle
Will **NOT** Do:

Run

Ride Horses

Look for
Adventure

Goat Girl told Merle that he could be a cowboy if he wanted to and proceeded to explain why with a persuasive thirty-minute audiovisual presentation.

It didn't work.

Listen, Goat Girl . . . for the last time, **I AM NOT A COWBOY!**

It was true Merle was not a cowboy, but as a young bull, that was his dream.

A dream he had
long forgotten.

A dream he didn't want
to remember.

Another humdrum day.

It would have stayed a humdrum day,
except something unusual was happening
on the farm.

The farmer had forgotten to close the chicken coop.

That was very un-humdrum.

The chickens forgot about laying extraordinarily average eggs and were overcome by the only thought a free-range chicken could have . . .

. . . crossing the road.

A dangerous road.

Goat Girl sprang into action to stop the chickens.

Merle did nothing.

Goat Girl tried to round them up with her horse.

Merle did nothing.

Goat Girl tried to distract them with her French cooking.

Merle still did nothing . . .

FREE SAMPLES

~~Chicken Specials!~~ Specials FOR Chickens!

LE HUMDRUM Cordon Bleu

. . . until he'd had enough.
It was time to do something.

HOWDY, LADIES.

Sorry to interrupt your trailblazin' adventures, but that road down yonder is closed.

I need to ask y'all to return to the farm in an orderly fashion.

Thank you kindly.

The next day, everything was back to being ho-hum on Humdrum Farm.

The chickens still laid extraordinarily average eggs.

The pigs rolled in the mud only when necessary, never for fun.

And the goats continued a diet of boring and bland food.

But if you were quiet and listened closely . . .

. . .the fields of Humdrum were
beating with a new sound.

One Goat Girl and one Cow Boy
(who was not a cowboy) . . .

Winfield Public Library
0S291 Winfield Road
Winfield, IL 60190
630-653-7599